D1303693

DATE DUE

MAY 2 3 2012			

Demco, Inc. 38-293

BABAR
A Gift for Mother

Illustrated by Judith Gray

Harry N. Abrams, Inc., Publishers

Celeste's children were excited because Mother's Day was coming.
At school, Pom made his mother a bowl out of clay.

Flora had saved her chore money for months. She bought Celeste a tiny glass horse.

Alexander chose a shiny silver balloon for his mother.

Isabelle had no present to give. She was too young to go to school and make something, and too little to do chores for money to buy a gift.

She decided to go talk to her father. Maybe he could help. She found Babar in his study.

"Come in!" he said, looking up from his work. Then he saw her face. "Isabelle, what's the matter?" he asked.

"Everybody has a present for Mother but me!" she said.

"Hmmm," said Babar. "Let's think about this. If you could give your mother anything, what would you give her?"

Isabelle remembered what her brothers and sister had done.
"I would give her a huge bowl made of gold," said Isabelle. "And silver, too. And diamonds."

"Very nice," said Babar. "And what else?"

"And a horse," said Isabelle. "A big pink one. And the bowl and the horse would be delivered by me, in a great big hot-air balloon."

"That sounds like a splendid Mother's Day present," said Babar.

"But I can't give her those things," said Isabelle sadly. "I'm too little."

"You're not too little for a lot of things," said Babar. "Maybe you could find a way to show your mother that you were thinking about her."

"I know!" cried Isabelle. "I can make her a picture! That's something I'm good at!"

Babar smiled. "Let's get out the crayons," he said.

Isabelle drew, and drew, and drew, and drew some more. She filled up the whole paper with color.

And when she was done . . . Ta-da!

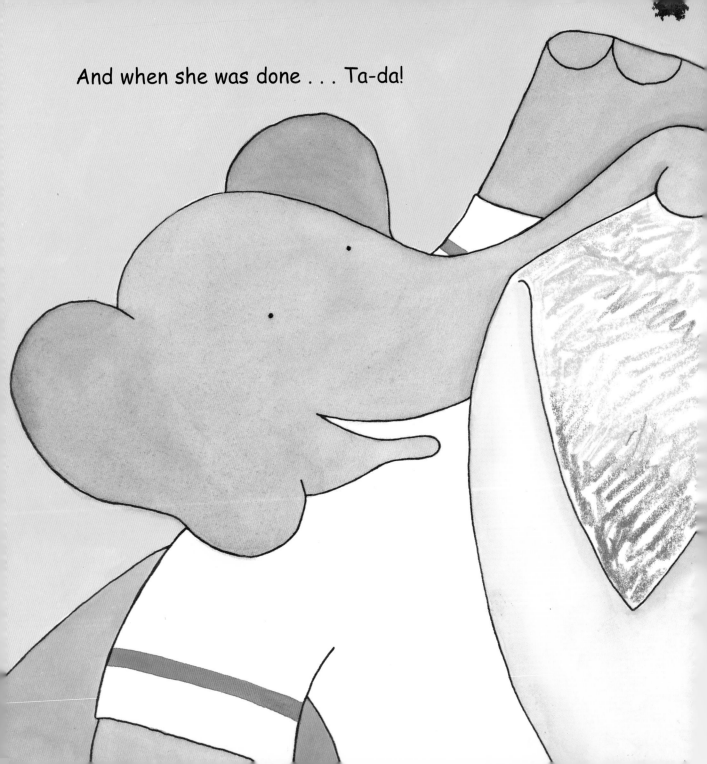

On Mother's Day, the family came together to celebrate.
First Pom gave Celeste the bowl he had made.

"What a magnificent bowl!" said Celeste. "I can see you worked very hard on it!"

"I did," said Pom.

Then Flora gave her the glass horse.

"How lovely!" said Celeste. "You must have saved your money for a long time."

"I did," said Flora.

Alexander gave her the shiny balloon.
"What a wonderful balloon!" said Celeste.
"You must have chosen it very carefully."
"I did," said Alexander.

Finally, it was Isabelle's turn.
Celeste untied the ribbon and
unrolled Isabelle's gift.

"Why, Isabelle, what a wonderful present!" said her mother.

"It's a gold and silver bowl and a pink horse," said Isabelle. "And there's me, bringing them to you in a hot-air balloon."

"It's marvelous," said Celeste. "I can see you thought about this gift a great deal!"

"I did," said Isabelle, beaming.

"Do you know what I think?" said Celeste. "I think I am the luckiest mother in the world!"

Designer: Celina Carvalho

Library of Congress Cataloging-in-Publication Data

Brunhoff, Laurent de, 1925–
Babar: a gift for Mother / Laurent de Brunhoff.
p. cm.
Summary: Each of Celeste's children has made or chosen a special gift
for Mother's Day except Isabelle, who describes to Babar what she would
like to give her mother and he finds a way to make it happen.
ISBN 0-8109-4837-0
[1. Mother's Day—Fiction. 2. Gifts—Fiction. 3. Elephants—Fiction.]
I. Title.
PZ7.B82843Baagf 2004
[E]—dc22
2003016753

Published in 2004 by Harry N. Abrams, Incorporated, New York.

Printed and bound in U.S.A.
10 9 8 7 6 5 4 3 2 1

Harry N. Abrams, Inc. 100 Fifth Avenue, New York, NY 10011
www.abramsbooks.com

Abrams is a subsidiary of
LA MARTINIÈRE
GROUPE